P9-DMZ-129

What are you eating, Alex?

"My brother and I will have the *escargot,*" Alex told the waiter.

The waiter raised his eyebrows. The other girls at the table exploded in laughter.

It wasn't long before the waiter returned and placed a steaming plate of food in front of Alex and one in front of Rudy.

"Do you know what you are eating?" Bryan whispered to Alex.

"No," Alex answered with a flip of her hair, "but whatever it is, it's good."

"Don't you want to know what it is?" Bryan hissed again.

"Yes, I guess so," replied Alex. She tried to appear confident, but really was beginning to feel quite uneasy.

Bryan spoke in a low voice, "It's . . ."

The ALEX Series
by Nancy Simpson Levene

- Shoelaces and Brussels Sprouts
- French Fry Forgiveness
- Hot Chocolate Friendship
- Peanut Butter and Jelly Secrets
- Mint Cookie Miracles
- Cherry Cola Champions
- The Salty Scarecrow Solution
- Peach Pit Popularity
- T-Bone Trouble
- Grapefruit Basket Upset
- Apple Turnover Treasure
- Crocodile Meatloaf
- Chocolate Chips and Trumpet Tricks
      —an Alex Devotional

Peach Pit Popularity

Nancy Simpson Levene

Chariot Books
A Division of Cook Communications

Chariot Books™ is an imprint of
David C. Cook Publishing Co.
David C. Cook Publishing Co., Elgin, Illinois 60120
David C. Cook Publishing Co., Weston, Ontario
Nova Distribution Ltd., Newton Abbot, England

PEACH PIT POPULARITY
© 1989 by Nancy R. Simpson for text and GraphCom
Corporation for interior illustrations.

All rights reserved. Except for brief excerpts for review
purposes, no part of this book may be reproduced or used
in any form without written permission from the publisher.

Cover design by Bill Paetzold
Cover illustration by Neal Hughes

First Printing, 1989
Printed in the United States of America
98 97 96 95 94 8 7 6 5 4

Library of Congress Cataloging-in-Publication Data
Levene, Nancy S., 1949-
Peach pit popularity / Nancy Simpson Levene; illustrated
by GraphCom Corporation.
p.   cm.
Summary: Vacationing at a lake, Alex learns about the
Christian values of love, patience, and goodness after
playing a practical joke on some "popular" girls who dress
and act alike and ridicule Alex for being an individual.
ISBN 1-55513-529-3
[1. Popularity—Fiction. 2. Individuality—Fiction. 3.
Vacations—Fiction. 4. Christian life—Fiction.] I. Morris,
Susan, ill. II. Title.
PZ7.L5726Pe   1989
[Fic]—dc20   89-33900
                                                              CIP
                                                              AC

*To Father God
who never fails
to rescue His children
and
To Patti and Lara Kupka,
special friends from the Lord
who remain strong and constant
in their love for us.*

You will know them by their fruits. Grapes are not gathered from thornbushes, nor figs from thistles, are they?

Even so every good tree bears good fruit; but the rotten tree bears bad fruit.

A good tree cannot produce bad fruit, nor can a rotten tree produce good fruit.

Every tree that does not bear good fruit is cut down, and thrown into the fire.

Matthew 7:16-19
New American Standard Bible

ACKNOWLEDGMENTS

Thank you, Mom and Dad, for your unfailing interest in Alex and for all your promotional efforts. Thank you, Lisa Schuver, for the *escargot* input, and Ed Marquette, for listening to all those fish stories. Again, thank you, Cara, for sharing your life with Alex.

CONTENTS

1 Rudy's Rescue 9

2 Eenie, Meenie, Mynie, Mo 21

3 Lost in the Woods 34

4 Water Ski Wrath 47

5 Peaches and Pits 58

6 More Trouble 67

7 Fish Heads in Bed 75

8 A Secret Swim 85

9 Rag Fight 98

10 Beach Party 109

CHAPTER 1

Rudy's Rescue

Alex knew there would be trouble the first time she saw the girls. Their hair was too pretty with the long, corkscrew curls so popular at school. Their clothes were too fashionably sloppy. Their socks matched their T-shirts. Their bracelets dazzled silver and green and fiery pink in the sun.

"See, Alex," said Mother as she pointed out the car window at the group of girls. "I told you there would be girls your age here."

Alex rolled her eyes skyward and sighed. Didn't her mother see how different she was from those girls?

"Ooooooh! Look at that beach!" cried Barbara, Alex's older sister. Barbara loved to sunbathe and, much to Alex's disgust, would spend hours in a lawn chair sunning by the swimming pool. There was no doubt about what her sister would do after they got out of the car.

"Stop, Dad, stop! I wanna see the lake!" hollered Rudy, Alex's younger brother. He was eight years old and yelled a lot in people's ears. Alex figured he would never stop yelling, not even when he grew up.

"There's the golf course." Mother pointed in another direction. "See, it says Crawdad Cove Golf Course."

"Great!" Father exclaimed. "This looks like a wonderful resort. I'm glad that George Anderson invited us to join them for a week."

George Anderson worked with Father at his law firm. Mr. Anderson had asked the Brackenburys to spend a week with him and his family at their favorite lakeside resort, Crawdad Cove. Other friends of the Andersons were also there.

"Hi, George," Father called out of the window as he pulled the Brackenbury station wagon into a nearby parking space. Father and Mother left the car and hurried over to talk to Mr. Anderson.

Alex followed her sister and brother out of the car. They gazed at the lake. It was beautifully blue and busy! Brightly colored sailboats and motorboats competed with each other for water space. Skiers made zig-zaggy lines across the water, while swimmers leaped or dove off docks that lined a marvelously big, sandy beach.

"Come on, Alex, let's go down to the beach." Rudy grabbed her hand and began to pull her down a little path to the lake.

"Wait a minute, Goblin," Alex replied. She turned and called to her parents, "We're going to the lake!"

"Don't fall in," her father called back.

"Very funny," Alex muttered as she followed Rudy down the path to the beach area. Barbara walked behind them.

"Hey, watch out! You almost hit me with that stupid snake again!" Alex shouted at Rudy. He had annoyed Barbara and Alex for the last several miles in the car by pretending to attack them with his rubber snake.

"You should have left that thing in the car," Barbara told Rudy. She was upset because Alex had tromped backwards onto her foot in trying to get out of the way of the snake.

Upon reaching the beach area, Alex noticed that the group of girls she had seen earlier was sitting on one of the long, wooden boardwalks that stretched out over the water. To Alex's dismay, Rudy ran onto that very boardwalk and marched right through the center of the group.

There was nothing else for Alex to do but follow Rudy. Barbara followed Alex. The three of them weaved their way in and around the girls.

"Excuse me," Alex said to each one of them, but she soon felt her neck and face blush red at their icy stares. Alex was intensely aware that her socks did not match her T-shirt, that she did not have a bracelet dangling from her wrist, and that her hair was brown, short, and straight.

A sudden scream from Rudy made Alex forget all about the girls. Her brother had run ahead and was leaning dangerously far out over the edge of the boardwalk. He was trying to reach something that floated in the water.

"My snake! It fell in the water!" Rudy cried.

"BRUSSELS SPROUTS, GOBLIN!" Alex hollered. "WATCH OUT! YOU'LL FALL IN!"

But her warning was too late. KER-SPLASH! Rudy's arms and legs flailed as he fell headfirst into the water.

"RUDY!" Barbara and Alex cried anxiously.

"HELP!" Rudy choked and sputtered and wildly thrashed the water. "My shoes are too heavy!" he gasped and sank underwater.

"What did he say?" Barbara asked Alex.

"His shoes are too heavy?" Alex replied, puzzled.

Rudy bobbed to the surface again but quickly sank back underneath.

"RUDY! RUDY!" Barbara screamed. "He's going to drown!"

Alex didn't need to hear any more. SPLASH! She jumped in the water close to her brother. Another SPLASH! and Barbara was in the water beside them.

"Quick! Grab his arm!" Barbara cried.

Alex caught hold of one of Rudy's arms and Barbara grasped the other. Together, they managed to keep Rudy's head above water.

"Now what do we do?" Alex spluttered. She and Barbara treaded water furiously on either side of Rudy.

"AHHHHHH!" Rudy shrieked. "I'm sinking!"

"No, you're not!" Barbara shouted in his ear. "We have you! We won't let you sink!"

"Ohhhhhh!" Rudy would not stop moaning. Alex could feel her legs tiring. She wondered how long they could keep him afloat.

"Do you think we could get him to the shore?" Alex called to her sister.

Barbara gazed at the beach. It was about one hundred feet away. "I don't think so," she called back.

"Rudy! Alex! Barbara!" a sudden familiar voice called. Father peered down from the dock at them. "Are you all right?" he asked them.

"No!" all three children answered at once.

"HELP, DAD, HELP!" Rudy shouted. He thrashed so wildly in the water that Alex and Barbara could not keep hold of him. His head sank under the water.

"RUDY!" they cried.

"Don't worry, I have him," said a calm voice. It seemed to come out of nowhere. Alex and Barbara gasped. A teenaged boy had popped up out of the water in between them. He flashed the girls a smile as he pulled Rudy above water with his strong arms.

Alex stared at the teenager. It was as if a blond Superman had come to rescue Rudy. His hair sparkled in the sun and his tanned arms and shoulders glistened. Alex thought she had never seen whiter teeth or bluer eyes.

With easy strokes, the teenager pulled Rudy around to the other side of the swimming dock.

"Come on," he called to Barbara and Alex. "There's a ladder over here."

Alex swam quickly to the ladder. Barbara followed more slowly. She seemed embarrassed. Alex could see no reason for Barbara to be embarrassed. Barbara had done a good thing by trying to save Rudy. So what if she had on her clothes instead of a swimming suit? Rudy should be the one who was embarrassed, and Alex let him know about it as soon as she

15

climbed up the ladder to the dock.

"Way to go, Goblin!" she shouted.

"Now, Alex," Mother said. "He's had a frightening experience. Let's try and be understanding."

Father put an arm around Alex. He shook hands with the blond teenager. "Thank you for rescuing my son," Father boomed.

"Oh, no problem," replied the boy. "I was glad to do it." He pointed at Rudy's feet. "His shoes are like anchors when they fill up with water."

Everyone stared at Rudy's shoes. They were high-top basketball shoes. They had already leaked quite a puddle around his feet.

Father laughed and bent over Rudy. He took off Rudy's shoes and poured the water out of each one.

"Are you staying here at Crawdad Cove, too?" Father asked the boy.

"Oh, yes, we got here yesterday," the boy replied. "My name's Matt Anderson."

"Then you must be George Anderson's oldest son," Father exclaimed. "It's nice to meet you. This is my son, Rudy, and my younger daughter, Alex. My older daughter, Barbara, is still in the water." Father called over the side of the dock, "Barbara, aren't you coming up here?"

"Uh, yeah, Dad, in a minute," came Barbara's hesitant voice from below.

"Well, what are you waiting for?" Father asked. "I want you to meet Matt."

Alex chuckled to herself. She was sure that Barbara was too embarrassed to meet Matt with dripping wet clothes and hair.

Father grew impatient. "Get out of the water,

17

Barbara, right now," he said sternly.

"Dad, I can't," Barbara replied in a low voice.

"What is the matter?" Father was irritated. He peered down at his oldest daughter, still treading water.

Alex looked down at Barbara, too. It only took a few seconds to realize that her sister indeed had a problem and should not come out of the water. It seemed that in the excitement of the rescue, Barbara's blouse had been ripped. She was desperately trying to hold it together in the water.

Father realized the situation at the same moment as Alex. "Oh, no!" he exclaimed. Alex watched his face turn bright red. "Stay there!" Father ordered Barbara.

"Don't worry, I'm not going anywhere!" Barbara replied.

"Young man," Father said to Matt, "my daughter needs a beach towel immediately. Would you have one handy?"

"Oh, sure," Matt replied. He ran down the boardwalk to the beach.

"Dad, I have to get out of here," Barbara pleaded. "I've swallowed so much lake water that I almost feel sick!"

"Okay, honey," Father soothed. "Matt should be here any minute with a towel."

Alex stared at the figures on the beach. She picked out Matt, sprinting along the sand back toward the boardwalk.

"Here he comes," Alex cried.

Matt quickly flipped the towel to Father. Father passed it to Alex who threw the towel down to Barbara. Barbara wrapped it around her shoulders, and Father helped her up the ladder.

"Well, hello there, young lady," a man strolling down the boardwalk said to Barbara. "I didn't see you there in the water."

"Thank goodness," Barbara muttered.

"What happened?" he asked Father. "Did she fall in?"

"Not exactly," Father replied. In his loud booming voice, he told the man how all three of his children had ended up in the lake.

He laughed as he listened to Father. Alex was

sure that everyone at the lake would hear the ridiculous story. To make matters worse, the group of girls on the boardwalk were listening to Father and pointing rudely at Alex. She looked down at the dock and tried to ignore their stares.

Finally, Alex and her family left the boardwalk and walked up a hill to one of the cottages overlooking the beach.

They were on the steps to the cottage when Rudy suddenly cried out, "My snake! We never got it out of the lake!"

"Good," Barbara told him. "I never want to see that snake again! It caused me enough trouble today."

"Right," Alex agreed. She looked back down the hill at the group of girls. "And I have a feeling that there will be more trouble before this week is over," she said to herself.

CHAPTER 2

Eenie, Meenie, Mynie, Mo . . .

That night, Alex's family walked to the Crawdad Cove restaurant for dinner. It seemed to be a popular place. It was very crowded inside.

"Hey, Brackenbury!" a man's voice called out to Father. "Come and join us at our table!"

It was Mr. Anderson. Father steered his family over to the Andersons' table. Barbara blushed deeply when she saw Matt Anderson sitting at the table. Matt smiled and pointed Barbara to an empty chair next to him. Then he grinned at Rudy and held up a rubber snake.

"My snake! You rescued him!" Rudy cried with joy. He ran to grab the snake.

Alex was just ready to plop down in a chair next to Barbara when Mr. Anderson spoke.

"I'm afraid there isn't quite enough room for everyone at this table. I was hoping that your two youngest children would join the table of children at the back of the room. My daughter and her friends are there and so is my youngest son, Bryan."

Mr. Anderson pointed to a long table at the very back of the restaurant. Seated at the table was the group of girls that Alex had seen earlier and one younger boy.

"Alex, you and Rudy would love to sit at that table with the other children, wouldn't you?" Mother asked.

"No," Alex answered.

"Ahem," Father cleared his throat. "Why not, Alex? The girls look like they are close to your age. I would think that you would have much more fun eating with them than eating with us old guys!"

The grown-ups at the table laughed. Alex knew she could not win against a table full of grown-ups. She was doomed to sit at the table with the group of girls.

"Come on, Alex," said Mrs. Anderson. "I'll

go with you and introduce you to the girls. That will make it easier, won't it?"

Alex shrugged her shoulders. She and Rudy followed Mrs. Anderson across the room. Alex's stomach was churning.

"Girls!" Mrs. Anderson got their attention as soon as she reached the table. "This is Alex. She is going to eat dinner with you this evening, along with her brother, Rudy."

There was a long hush at the table. All eyes were turned on Alex. She could see no friendly ones except perhaps the eyes belonging to the younger Anderson boy. Alex wished she could hide under the table.

"This is my daughter, Lisa," said Mrs. Anderson and laid her hand on the shoulder of a pretty girl with long, blond curls. "And next to her is Emily," Mrs. Anderson went on, "and over there is Elena, and . . ."

Alex lost track of the names of the girls after the first two or three were introduced to her. The girls were far more dressed up than she was—some even wore eye makeup. She was aware of the rude pokes, jabs, and giggles that they threw at one another. There was no doubt that the girls were making fun of her.

When Mrs. Anderson finished the introductions, Alex sat down in an empty chair. She did not look at the girls, but stared at Rudy as he sat down next to her and across from Bryan Anderson.

"Would you care to order, Miss?" A sudden voice spoke above Alex's left ear.

Alex jumped in her chair and twisted her neck around to see a tall, unsmiling waiter standing behind her chair.

"Order?" Alex repeated as if she had never heard the word before.

"Yes," the waiter replied stiffly. "Would you care to order your dinner?"

"Oh, yeah, sure," Alex mumbled. "Uh, what do you have?"

The waiter sighed, "I'll get you a menu." He hurried away. The girls snickered.

After he had returned, Alex stared at the menu in confusion. She had never heard of most of the dishes on the menu. What was "Boston Scrod" or "Kiwi Orange Roughy"? She couldn't ask the girls. They would only laugh at her. And she certainly wasn't going to ask that crabby old waiter.

"What do you want to eat?" Alex whispered to Rudy.

"A hamburger," Rudy answered quickly.

"I don't think they have them here, Goblin," Alex told her brother. "Look at the menu."

Rudy stared at the menu. "I can't read any of this stuff!" he declared.

"Neither can I," Alex whispered. "We just have to pick something and hope it's good."

"Okay," Rudy replied. He began to chant and point at each dinner item, "Eenie, meenie, mynie, mo . . ."

Alex cringed behind the menu and endured the teasing looks and giggles from the other girls. She knew, of course, that this was not the proper way to select a meal from a menu.

"My mother told me to pick the very best one and y-o-u are it!" Rudy finished his chant at the exact moment that the waiter returned to stand behind Alex. His finger had selected something called *escargot*.

"My brother will have the *escargot*," Alex told the waiter. She scanned the menu once more. "And I believe I'll have the same thing." She tried to speak in her most confident and grown-up manner.

The waiter raised his eyebrows. The girls at the table exploded in laughter and poked and jabbed each other even more than before.

Alex turned sideways in her chair and ignored everyone. Her face burned with embarrassment. Why were they laughing at her? What had she done that was so wrong?

Blinking back hot tears, Alex stared over the top of Rudy's head. On the wall, right above Rudy, hung a picture of a blue whale. Alex looked at the picture without even seeing it.

"Do you like whales or something?" a boyish voice suddenly asked her.

Startled, Alex jerked her head around and found herself staring into the second set of the bluest eyes she had ever seen. It was Bryan Anderson. He looked almost like a carbon copy of his older brother, Matt.

"What did you say?" Alex asked uncertainly.

"You were staring at that picture on the wall for so long," Bryan jerked his thumb at the blue whale picture, "that I thought you might like whales or something."

"Oh." Alex focused on the picture for the first time. "Uh, not really."

Bryan smiled and reached his arm across the table to shake hands with Alex and Rudy. Alex smiled in relief. It was so nice to see a friendly face at the table.

It wasn't long before the waiter returned and placed a steaming plate of food in front of Alex and one in front of Rudy. The plates looked very interesting. Each was divided into six sections—five around the outside and one in the middle. It reminded Alex of a wagon wheel with spokes and a hub in the middle. Each section was filled with chunks of something.

"What is it?" Rudy asked Alex.

"I don't know," Alex whispered. Trying to act unconcerned, she dug one of the chunks out of the middle section of her plate and popped it into her mouth.

"Oooooh, it's hot," Alex warned Rudy. She quickly sipped her water. "Ummm, it's not too bad," she added. "It's some kind of fish with a lot of garlic on it."

"Garlic?" Rudy asked suspiciously.

"Yeah, you know, the stuff that Mom dumps on spaghetti," Alex replied.

Rudy's face brightened. He, too, popped a chunk into his mouth.

For some reason, this made the girls at the other end of the table laugh louder than ever. Alex grew angry. After all, she and Rudy were quietly eating their dinner and behaving themselves. Didn't those girls know how to act in a restaurant? Well, she would show them. With a flip of her hair, Alex ate another bite using her absolute best table manners.

"Do you know what you are eating?" Bryan Anderson leaned across the table and whispered to Alex.

"No." Alex flipped her hair again. "But whatever it is, it's good."

"Don't you want to know what it is?" Bryan hissed again.

"Yes, I guess so," replied Alex. She tried to appear confident, but really was beginning to feel quite uneasy.

"Snails," Bryan said in a low voice.

Alex dropped her fork. It clattered to the floor. "What did you say?" she asked Bryan.

"Snails!" he repeated, louder. "You are eating SNAILS!"

Rudy made a gagging sound. Alex stared at her brother for a moment. "Excuse me," she said to no one in particular and ran from the table to the outside door of the restaurant.

On her way, Alex heard the uproarious

laughter of the girls at her table. She also thought she heard her mother call her name. But Alex didn't stop. She couldn't stop. She felt sick . . . oh, so sick . . . and she had to reach the door before . . . before . . .

Alex stumbled outside but did not get past the front steps before getting violently sick to her stomach. She was dimly aware of Rudy beside her, also sick to his stomach.

It wasn't long before Alex felt her mother's touch as she gently helped Alex and Rudy walk down the steps of the restaurant. Alex leaned on her mother's arm as they slowly walked to their cottage. She could hear Father in the background apologizing to Mr. Anderson for having to leave the restaurant so early. She also heard Barbara call good-bye to Matt Anderson. Alex shuddered. She never wanted to see those people again. Not after tonight!

"What in the world happened to you two?" Mother asked Alex and Rudy as soon as they were inside the cottage. Father and Barbara had also come in and were staring with puzzled faces at Alex and Rudy.

Alex covered her face and moaned. She could not even say the word.

"SNAILS!" Rudy said it for her. "We ate snails!"

"You ate snails?" Father repeated with a puzzled look. "What are you talking about?"

"In the restaurant," Alex tried to explain. "Rudy and I couldn't read the menu so we just picked something. . . ."

"Yeah, I went 'eenie, meenie, mynie, mo,' " Rudy interrupted.

"And what we picked turned out to be snails," Alex finished. She made a face and moaned again.

"How do you know it was snails?" Father asked.

"Because Bryan Anderson told us so," answered Rudy.

"How did it read on the menu?" Father questioned them.

"E-S-C-A-R-G-O-T," Alex and Rudy spelled out loud.

"That's snails all right," sighed Father.

"It was horrible!" Alex exclaimed. "The

whole dinner was just horrible." She told her family about the rude girls at the table and how they had laughed at her and Rudy. "They must have known what *escargot* was and they didn't even tell us. They thought it was funny that Rudy and I ordered snails!"

"Oh, I'm so sorry," said Mother and hugged Alex tightly.

"Even if the girls didn't tell you, the waiter should have told you what *escargot* was," Father said.

"Well, he didn't," Alex sniffed. "He was mean, too."

"It looks like the waiter is getting what he deserves," Barbara said all of a sudden. She was looking out the front window of the cottage.

"Huh? What do you mean?" Alex asked her sister.

"It looks like the waiter has to clean up the steps," Barbara giggled.

They all hurried to join Barbara at the window. Sure enough, the same waiter who had served Alex and Rudy was outside with a bucket and a mop.

"I bet from now on he tells children what *escargot* means," Rudy commented.

"I bet he does!" Father agreed, and they all laughed together.

CHAPTER 3

Lost in the Woods

The next morning Rudy stood outside the cottage door and called to Alex, "Come on outside, Alex! Those creepy girls aren't out here. Nobody's out here."

"Shhhhh, Goblin!" Alex hissed out of a window. "Somebody might hear you."

"Aw, come on, Alex," Rudy whined. "Come outside with me."

"Oh, okay," Alex agreed. She did not really want to stay inside the cottage all day—not with a beautiful, big lake just outside the door. But, at the same time, she did not want to see any of those girls again. Not after last night!

Poking her nose outside the door, Alex looked in all directions. It looked safe so she stepped out onto the porch. Those girls probably sleep until noon, she told herself. Just like Miss Mushy.

"Let's go down to the lake," Rudy suggested.

Crossing the swimming beach, Alex and Rudy passed the boardwalk where Rudy had dropped his rubber snake in the water the day before. Alex giggled when she remembered how they had all jumped into the water and the trouble that Barbara had in getting out of the water.

"You know, so far this vacation has been really embarrassing for all of us," Alex commented to Rudy.

"It has?" Rudy asked.

"Sure, you fell in the lake yesterday with your clunky shoes on," Alex reminded her brother.

"Oh, yeah," Rudy grinned sheepishly.

"And all three of us ended up in the water with our clothes on," Alex went on, "and Barbara couldn't get out of the water without Matt bringing her a towel . . ."

"And getting sick last night at the restaurant," Rudy interrupted.

"That was the worst," Alex sighed.

Laughing, the brother and sister walked past the dock and on down the shoreline. They counted the sailboats on the lake and watched two of them race. They skipped rocks out across the water. Moving farther and farther from the beach and the cluster of cottages, Alex and Rudy began to pick up interesting rocks of all shapes and sizes. Soon, their pockets were bulging.

"Let's put all of our rocks in a pile on the ground. Then we can come back later and get them," Alex suggested.

"Good idea," said Rudy. "I can't walk with all of these rocks in my pockets."

The children emptied their pockets and stashed their rocks at the base of a large tree. Alex picked the tree because it was the tallest one in sight and should be easy to find again.

"Hey look!" Alex exclaimed, pointing a little way beyond the tree. The ground suddenly dropped off, forming a deep ditch or gully. A stream of water lazily flowed down the middle of the gully. Large willow and other trees grew along the banks of the stream.

"Awesome!" Rudy breathed. "Let's go!" He and Alex raced down the sides of the gully to the stream. They splashed through it, hopping from rock to rock.

"Tadpoles!" Alex soon cried with delight. She and Rudy busily went about catching the small creatures. They made a "swimming pool" for the tadpoles in one area of the stream and tried to keep the creatures in the pool.

The tadpoles, however, would not stay in their swimming pool. No matter how many rocks Rudy would pile up or how thick Alex would build the walls with mud, the tadpoles would somehow wriggle out to other parts of the stream.

Finally, hot and tired, the children sat down to rest in the shade of the umbrella-like branches of a large willow tree.

"This would be a perfect place for a picnic," Alex observed, looking at the crisscross pattern of leaves above her. She listened as her stomach rumbled noisily.

"I'm hungry," Rudy decided.

"It must be way past lunchtime," Alex guessed. "We'd better go back. I bet Mom and Dad are looking for us."

"They would never find us here," Rudy observed.

Alex looked up at the top of the gully. She could not see the lake at all from where she was sitting. *Rudy's right,* she thought to herself. *We are hidden. No one on the lake could see us.*

A small chill of fear passed through Alex. What if they were lost in the gully forever? "Come on," she said to Rudy, standing up quickly. "Let's get out of here."

They quickly climbed one side of the gully and were soon standing above it. Alex breathed a sigh of relief. There was the lake stretching out before them, blue and shimmering in the sun.

But the smile on Alex's face quickly disappeared. Something was wrong! The woods hadn't been this thick or so close to the water. And where was the tall tree with their pile of rocks? It wasn't anywhere in sight.

"Do you think we came up the wrong side of the gully?" Alex asked Rudy.

"We must have." Rudy sounded worried. "This doesn't look right at all."

Suddenly, a loud crash sounded behind them.

They spun around but could see nothing.

"Maybe it was just a falling tree branch," said Alex, trying to sound brave.

"Maybe," Rudy answered with a shaky voice, "or it could have been a bear or something."

"That's ridiculous, Goblin," Alex replied. "There aren't any bears here."

"How do you know?" Rudy challenged.

Alex ignored the question. "Come on," she said, "let's try to find our way back to the cottages."

They ran back to the gully and crossed to the other side. Climbing up the slope, Alex hoped with all of her heart that they would see a familiar landmark.

"Brussels sprouts!" she cried upon reaching the top.

"What?" Rudy asked anxiously.

"This isn't right either! Look, the lake is all around us." She pointed in several directions. "It looks like we're on an island or something. How can that be?"

"What are we going to do?" wailed Rudy.

"Let me think," Alex said, shushing her brother. "I don't want to go back to the gully because every time we do, we seem to get more lost. I guess we ought to follow the shoreline. It's gotta lead us to the cottages eventually."

Alex and Rudy trudged along the shore of the lake for what seemed like hours and hours. The land became wilder and rougher. They had to scramble over fallen trees and squeeze through tangled undergrowth.

Finally, Rudy could go no further. "I'm too tired," he told Alex.

"Okay, Goblin," agreed Alex. She was also exhausted. "Let's go sit on those big rocks close to the water. That way, if a boat comes by, somebody will see us."

"Do you think a boat will come by?" Rudy asked as soon as they were settled on top of a large boulder.

"Oh, I'm pretty sure one will come along," Alex answered. She tried to sound confident for Rudy's sake, but really, Alex was very worried. They must be a very long way from the cottages, she thought. They had seen no sign of a house or any other building. "Oh, please, Lord Jesus," Alex silently prayed, "help us."

"I'm thirsty," Rudy suddenly complained. "It's awful to have to sit and stare at all this water and not be able to drink any of it."

"I know," Alex agreed, "but you know how Mom says never to drink lake water. It will make you sick."

"Just a little bit?" Rudy pleaded. "Can't I drink just a little bit?"

"You don't want to get sick, Goblin," Alex exclaimed. "Just think how bad it would be if you were lost, hungry, thirsty, *and* sick! Don't you remember how it felt to be sick last night?"

"Yuck." Rudy groaned and held his stomach. "I guess you're right."

After awhile, the children lay flat on their backs on the boulder. They stretched out their tired legs and stared at the clouds skimming the sky. The warm sun made them sleepy and soon they dozed.

All at once, Alex sat up wide awake. She felt the hair rise on the back of her neck. Little shivers ran up and down her back. She felt that something was watching her!

Turning around, Alex scanned the bank. She caught her breath. There, in the shadows, half hidden by leaves and bark, crouched a dog. Or was it a wolf?

For what seemed like forever, Alex and the wolf-dog stared at one another. Not even when Rudy awoke and called out Alex's name, did Alex take her eyes away from the animal.

"Quiet, Goblin, don't make any sudden moves," she warned in a low voice.

"What's the matter?" Rudy asked, alarmed.

"We have company," Alex replied quietly. She pointed at the trees on the bank.

"Who?" Rudy shouted and sat up.

"Shhhh," Alex hissed. "We don't want to disturb him."

"Disturb who?" Rudy whispered.

"Over there." Alex continued to point at the first row of trees on the bank. "Can't you see him?"

"Oh," Rudy breathed. "It's a dog. Here, boy! Come here, boy!" Rudy whistled for the animal to come.

"Rudy!" Alex cried in alarm. The wolf-dog had stood up at Rudy's whistle and looked keenly at the children. Alex pulled her brother down beside her. "Don't do that," she warned. "We don't know if he's friendly."

The children sat on the rock and stared at the animal. Finally, Rudy got restless and began to skip little rocks across the surface of the lake. He then picked up a stick and threw it out as far as he could over the water.

"Uh-oh," Alex gasped. The second that Rudy had thrown the stick, the wolf-dog had suddenly bounded out from the trees and had run straight toward them.

Just as Alex was sure that the animal meant to eat them for dinner, it sprang around them and into the water. It swam hard and fast to the place where Rudy's stick had splashed into the water. Grabbing the stick in its teeth, the wolf-dog turned and swam back to the children.

"He fetched my stick!" Rudy laughed.

"Brussels sprouts," was all Alex could say.

Climbing up on a nearby rock, the wolf-dog began to gnaw on the stick. It watched the

children out of the corner of its eye.

This time, Alex picked up a stick. WHOOSH! She flung it out across the lake. SPLASH! The animal was after it.

Time and time again, the children threw sticks for the wolf-dog to fetch. In the fun of it all, Alex and Rudy ended up in the lake themselves, but as Rudy put it, that cooled them off and made them "less thirsty."

Finally, all three of them collapsed on the giant rocks. Alex and Rudy shrieked and giggled when the wolf-dog shook itself dry, spraying them with drops of cold water.

"He's a neat dog," Rudy said as the animal lay down beside them.

"Yeah," Alex agreed. She stared at it up close. She couldn't decide if it was a dog or a wolf. *I guess it doesn't matter as long as he's friendly,* she told herself.

Alex, Rudy, and the wolf-dog stretched themselves out on the warm rocks. After so much excitement, it felt good to relax.

Alex didn't remember closing her eyes, but when she opened her eyes much later, it was pitch black!

"Brussels sprouts!" she gasped.

Groping in the darkness, Alex tried to find Rudy. She was afraid of slipping off the rock and falling into the water below. But what if Rudy had rolled off the rock in his sleep?

Cold fear spread through Alex. Tears began to roll down her cheeks. "Please, Lord Jesus," she sobbed, "help me!"

"Alex?" cried a frightened voice next to her right ear.

"Rudy!" Alex grabbed her brother and

pulled him next to her.

"Alex, I'm scared," Rudy whimpered.

"So am I, Goblin," admitted Alex. She wondered if the wolf-dog was still close to them. What if it turned into a dangerous animal at night? What if it was right now crouching—ready to spring on them?

Shivers traveled up and down Alex's back. She tried her best to control her fear. But she and Rudy were lost. And it was so dark!

"Alex," Rudy said in a small voice. "I think we need to pray."

"Right, Goblin," Alex agreed. "Lord Jesus, please help us. Please help someone to find us."

Soon Alex heard a sound that made hope leap back into her heart. Was it the sound of an engine? Yes, Alex was sure it was the sound of an engine. A boat must be coming their way!

"Goblin, do you hear that?" Alex asked excitedly. "I think a boat is coming! We're going to be rescued!"

CHAPTER 4

Water Ski Wrath

Alex strained her ears. There was that noise again! It sounded just like the chug-whir of a motorboat engine. And it was getting closer. But would it get close enough for someone to see them?

Soon, a beam of light bounced over the water in front of Alex and Rudy. The dark outline of a boat came into view.

"HELP!" the children called as loud as they could. "HELP! HELP!"

The beam of light swung and flashed over the rocks where Alex and Rudy were huddled. She heard a man say, "Over there! By those rocks!" Her heart leaped for joy when she heard her father shout, "Alex? Is that you?"

Alex opened her mouth to answer her father

but, to her surprise, found that she could not make a sound. She was crying too hard!

It was Rudy who jumped to his feet, leaned dangerously far out over the rocks, and called to his father. It took all of Alex's strength to keep him from diving into the water in front of the oncoming boat.

Because of the rocks, the boat had to stop several yards away from them. Alex watched her father jump from the boat and leap from rock to rock, making his way toward her and Rudy. She was amazed at how fast her father moved over the rocks and through the water. It was comforting to know that soon his arms would lift her up and she would be safe—safe from the darkness, safe from the water, safe from everything.

Making one final leap, Father reached the children. He caught them both into his arms. Alex heard her father whisper, "Thank You, God," over and over. She felt his warm tears on her cheek. He smiled at her and she knew that his love for her ran far deeper than any words could ever say.

Father helped Alex and Rudy over the rocks to the boat. The children met another man waiting for them in the boat. He was a park ranger who regularly patrolled the lake and woods.

To Alex the boat ride was long and bumpy. She was anxious to see her mother and to get safely inside the cottage. She had had enough adventure for one day.

The dock at Crawdad Cove was full of people waiting for news of the children. When they arrived, Alex and Rudy found themselves the center of attention. Everyone hugged and kissed them—even people they didn't know! Alex noticed that the group of snobby girls was there. Of course, they said nothing to Alex.

"I knew God would bring you back to me!" Mother cried as she held Alex and Rudy close.

"When we were by ourselves on the rocks in the dark," Alex told her mother, "we asked the Lord to help us and right after that, the boat came."

Mother smiled. "God knows how to rescue His children."

Alex and Rudy told their parents and the park ranger about their adventures. The ranger was particularly interested in the wolf-dog.

"I think I've seen that animal before in those woods," the ranger drawled.

"Well, if you see him again, don't shoot him," Alex told the ranger. "He was really nice to me and Rudy."

"Yeah," Rudy added. "He was our friend!"

"Okay," the ranger chuckled. "I'm glad you told me about him."

The next morning, Alex and Rudy slept late. They slept so late that when they finally awoke, Mother was fixing lunch instead of breakfast.

"Guess what?" Father announced when he came in from outside. "Mr. Anderson is going to take you waterskiing this afternoon."

"Oh, boy!" the children cried.

That afternoon, they hurried down to the boat dock. Father went with them.

"Climb aboard!" Mr. Anderson waved to them from a bright red motorboat. Alex's heart sank. At the very back of the boat sat two girls.

Alex recognized them as Lisa Anderson and her friend Emily. They had made fun of Alex the night she and Rudy had eaten the *escargot*.

"Alex, why don't you sit with Lisa and Emily?" Mr. Anderson suggested. He asked Rudy to sit with Bryan in the middle seat. Father sat by Mr. Anderson up front.

At first, Lisa and Emily would not make room for Alex to sit on the backseat with them. Alex stood awkwardly clinging to the side of the boat while Mr. Anderson backed the boat out of the dock.

"Alex, you must sit down in the boat," Mr. Anderson called loudly.

"Uh, excuse me," Alex said to Emily and Lisa. She somehow managed to squeeze herself in beside Emily on the backseat. The girls giggled.

Alex hated that boat ride! It did not matter that Mr. Anderson drove the boat at a marvelously fast pace or that the fresh, crisp breeze blew in her face. Alex was cramped and uncomfortable, but most of all, she was terribly hurt and confused.

Why are the girls being so mean? she wondered. She hadn't done anything to them. She wished she had never come. Going waterskiing for the first time was not worth this kind of treatment.

The boat slowed and stopped. Alex looked around. They had come a long way from the dock. The beach and cottages looked like tiny specks in the distance.

"Lisa," Mr. Anderson called to his daughter, "you go first so Alex and Rudy can see how you get up on the skis."

"Emily and I want to ski double," Lisa hollered to her father.

"Okay, okay." Mr. Anderson waved his hand. "You and Emily get in the water." He threw two pairs of skis overboard.

As the girls got ready to ski, Mr. Anderson told Alex and Rudy all about skiing and how they should hold the tow rope and keep the tips of the skis up out of the water at takeoff.

Lisa signaled to her father that she and Emily were ready. The engine roared and Mr. Anderson took off at top speed. Alex watched as Lisa and Emily were pulled up on top of the water.

"Awesome!" Alex gasped. She forgot her hurt feelings and waited impatiently for it to be her turn.

Lisa and Emily skied in and out of the wake of waves at the back of the boat. They moved forward to ski on either side of the boat and then dropped behind the boat to join hands. Alex was impressed. They looked like pros.

After two trips around the lake, Mr. Anderson cut the boat's speed and it slowed and stopped. Lisa and Emily sank to the surface of the water.

"It's Alex's turn!" Mr. Anderson shouted.

"No!" Lisa complained to her father. "I didn't get to practice skiing backwards."

"You can do that another time," her father replied. "Let Alex have a turn."

"Come on, Dad, please," Lisa whined. "Let me ski backwards one time."

"Oh, all right." Mr. Anderson gave in. Alex sank back in her seat disappointed. She knew that Lisa and Emily would do their best to keep her from waterskiing.

The boat sped off. It wasn't long this time, however, before both girls fell into the waves as they tried to ski backwards.

"Alex's turn!" Mr. Anderson shouted again.

Lisa and Emily grumbled but climbed back into the boat. Alex took her place in the water. It was freezing cold, but she did not care.

"Lisa, pass your skis down to Alex," Mr. Anderson directed his daughter.

"Sure, Dad," Lisa replied. She hoisted the skis over the side of the boat and shoved them in the opposite direction from Alex.

"Lisa!" Her father frowned.

"Sorry, Dad," Lisa shrugged, "the skis slipped." She giggled at Emily.

By the time Alex chased the skis through the water and pulled them back behind the boat, she was so angry that she did not even listen to Mr. Anderson's last-minute instructions. With a scowl on her face, she held the tips of her skis out of the water and waited for the boat to speed off. She ignored the anxious look on her father's face as he peered overboard at her.

The boat shot forward. The rope jerked as it

pulled Alex through the water. Slowly, Alex stood up on the skis, her arm and leg muscles fighting to keep her balance. With sheer determination, Alex forced herself to stand upright on the skis. She was not going to fall in front of Lisa and Emily!

After the first few minutes, Alex began to relax and feel more confident on the skis. She even risked grinning at her father and brother. They were waving happily at her from inside the boat. Alex did not dare to take a hand off the rope to wave back at them. Not this time anyway.

Oh, this is so fantastic! she told herself. Why, she could ski for hours and hours. She hoped Mr. Anderson would give her a long, long ride.

All of a sudden, Alex realized that Lisa and Emily were waving at her and trying to get her attention. They were making strange gestures. Alex squinted to try and see what they were doing. It almost looked like Emily was getting sick to her stomach right there in the back of the boat! Then, suddenly, Alex understood. Emily was making fun of Alex by reminding her how she had gotten sick in the restaurant the other night!

Even with the cold wind and spray hitting her, Alex felt her face getting hot. She blinked back angry tears and jerked her head to one side. Those disgusting girls! She did not want to look at them ever again!

In her anger, Alex forgot to concentrate on skiing and, quite suddenly, lost her balance. The skis slid out from under her and Alex hit the water hard, the rope dragging her several yards before her mind screamed for her to let go. Completely waterlogged, Alex sank under the waves.

CHAPTER 5

Peaches
and Pits

With her lungs about to burst, Alex struggled to get to the surface of the water. The lake water was so dark that she could not tell which way was up and which was down. Panic began to spread through her whole body.

Strong arms suddenly grabbed her and pulled her to the surface. Alex squinted bleary-eyed into the face of her father.

"Are you all right, Firecracker?" Father asked, using his special nickname for Alex.

"Yeah," Alex gasped. She let him help her back into the boat. She squeezed in beside him on the front seat.

"You did real well until you fell, Alex," Mr. Anderson told her with a smile.

"I wouldn't have fallen if those bratty girls

hadn't made faces at me," Alex said under her breath.

She stared straight ahead and did not turn around once for the rest of the boat ride—not even when Rudy took his turn waterskiing.

When they returned to the dock, Alex climbed out of the boat, thanked Mr. Anderson, and walked stiffly back to the cottage.

Once inside, Alex let all of the anger and hurt explode with one gigantic kick at the wall. She collapsed in tears on the floor.

"Alex!" Mother exclaimed, running over to her. "What is wrong?"

"It's not fair! It's not fair!" Alex sobbed.

"What's not fair?" asked Mother.

"Those girls were awful mean to her," Rudy answered, coming to stand beside Mother and Alex.

"What girls?" Mother wanted to know.

"Lisa Anderson and her friend Emily," Father said, entering the cottage. He and Rudy told Mother all that had happened.

"Oh, dear," sighed Mother. "I was hoping that Alex would become friends with the girls."

"I'm sorry, Mom." Alex hung her head. "But every time I meet a bunch of girls like that—you know, the popular kind of girls—I can't seem to get along with them. They don't like me, and, well, sometimes I think there must be something wrong with me!" Alex burst into tears.

"Oh, Alex, that's not true," Mother exclaimed and hugged Alex tightly.

"There's nothing wrong with you, Firecracker," Father said gently. "But there is something wrong with that group of girls."

"There is?" sniffled Alex.

"Yes, they are eating bad food," Father replied.

"Eating bad food?" Alex frowned. "What does food have to do with it?"

"Let me see if I can explain what I mean," said Father. "First, let's pretend that everyone in the world is a fruit tree and that we are all planted in one big orchard. Let's see, what kind of fruit trees shall we be?" he asked Rudy.

"Peach trees," Rudy decided.

"Okay," chuckled Father. "We are peach

trees. Now, there are two different sections in the orchard. In one section, the trees are planted in God's rich soil and drink God's mineral water. They enjoy God's beautiful sunshine and grow to be healthy, beautiful trees." Father held his arms up high and pretended to be a tall, healthy tree.

Alex chuckled at her father. He made a rather funny-looking tree.

"But in the other section of the orchard," Father went on, "the poor trees are planted in rocky soil that does not have enough nutrients to feed the trees properly. There is also a shortage of water. So the trees look like this." Father bent over and let his arms droop like a twisted, unhealthy tree.

Alex and Rudy laughed out loud at their father. He looked twice as funny as before.

"I hope you don't get stuck in that position," warned Mother.

"Ahem," Father cleared his throat and straightened himself to a normal position. He looked at Alex. "Which trees do you think grow the best peaches? The ones in God's section of

the orchard or the ones in the other section?"

"The trees in God's section, of course," replied Alex with a smile. "I bet the peaches from the yucky, droopy trees are rotten."

"Oooooh yeah," whistled Rudy. "I bet all that's left of them are a bunch of pits!"

The rest of the family laughed.

"What would you say if I told you that, just like the trees in the orchard, you and I produce fruit, too?" Father asked them as soon as they had quieted down.

"Huh?" Rudy looked puzzled. "We don't

have any fruit growing on us.''

Alex giggled as she tried to imagine big, juicy peaches hanging from Rudy's arms.

Father smiled. ''Think of the fruit that we produce as being our achievements in life. For example, if we help other people, then we have grown the fruit of kindness. Or, if we share something with other people, then we have grown the fruit of unselfishness. The Bible talks a lot about fruit. In Galatians 5:22 and 23, there is a whole list of what the Bible calls 'the fruit of the Holy Spirit.' ''

''Brussels sprouts,'' Alex exclaimed. ''I didn't know that.''

''Do you remember why the trees in God's section of the orchard grew good fruit?'' Father asked.

''Sure,'' Rudy answered. ''The trees in God's section had better soil and water.''

''Exactly,'' Father agreed. ''Those trees had the perfect kind of food, and that food made it possible for them to grow good fruit. In our case, we also need the perfect kind of food to grow good fruit. Can you guess what it is?''

Alex and Rudy looked at each other and shrugged. What was Father talking about—a perfect kind of food?

Finally, Rudy guessed. "Turkey and dressing and cranberries," he said, thinking of his favorite holiday meal.

Father and Mother laughed.

"Good guess, Rudy," chuckled Father, "but I'm not talking about food that you eat with your mouth."

"What other kind of food is there?" Rudy asked, confused.

"Spiritual food," replied his father.

"Oh, I know!" shouted Alex. "It's the Bible!"

"The Bible!" Rudy frowned at his sister. "You can't eat the Bible!"

Alex giggled. "Rudy, I didn't mean that you actually eat the pages."

Father smiled. "Alex is right," he said. "The Bible is God's spiritual food for us. By reading it, we feed our minds and our spirits with the very thoughts of God. That helps us to produce good fruit. Jesus tells us that we will know if a person is good or bad by the kind of fruit he or she produces."

"What about Lisa and Emily?" Alex asked her father. "They produced bad fruit by being mean to me. Does that mean they are eating bad food?"

"Hmmmm," Father rubbed his chin. "I would say that Lisa and Emily are eating the worldly popularity food."

"The worldly popularity food?" Alex exclaimed. "What's that?"

"That's believing you have to dress a certain way, talk a certain way, and act a certain way to be popular," Father answered.

"That sounds like that whole group of girls," Alex giggled. "They all look alike."

"Yes," agreed Father, "but the worst is that they will say or do anything their friends want them to even if it hurts someone else."

"Like me," said Alex.

"Right," said Father.

"If hurting others is the fruit that comes from being popular, then I don't want to be popular," declared Alex.

"Just remember, Firecracker, that there are two sides to the orchard," Father reminded her. "You can be popular with God and with other Christians. Choose your friends carefully."

"Yeah," Rudy suddenly interrupted. "Choose the peaches and not the pits!"

They all laughed together.

CHAPTER 6

More Trouble

That evening, Alex and Rudy sat in the Crawdad Cove Restaurant at a table with their parents. They had not been back to the restaurant since Alex had ordered *escargot* two nights before.

"Uh, Dad," Alex said, "will you help me figure out the stuff on the menu? I can't read it because it has too many fish names."

Just then a waiter passed their table. It was the same waiter who had waited on Alex and had washed the steps outside the restaurant two nights ago. Alex quickly ducked behind her menu.

"Alex, I cannot talk to you when your menu is covering your head," Father told her.

Alex peeked around a corner of the menu.

The waiter was at the far end of the room. She laid her menu down.

"Dad, you better help her order," Rudy piped up. "We sure don't want to eat snails again!"

"Shhhhh!" Alex hissed at Rudy. She looked around to see if anyone had heard him.

Father and Mother laughed. Then they helped Alex and Rudy decide what to order from the menu.

"May I take your order?" The waiter suddenly appeared at the table.

Alex threw a napkin over her head and slid down in her chair until she was practically under the table. Father sighed and ordered Alex's dinner for her.

The waiter left the table and Alex sat up in her chair. Soon Alex found herself staring at the table of girls at the other end of the restaurant. *They must eat together every night,* she thought. She wished she had a friend with her. Things would be so much better if her best friend, Janie, had come along.

Quite suddenly, Lisa Anderson looked up

and caught Alex staring at her. She poked Emily and the two of them smirked and pointed at Alex. Alex turned her head away, but she knew that their sudden burst of laughter was meant for her. Her cheeks burned with embarrassment.

Why are they so mean? Alex cried to herself. She pounded the table with her fist. Unfortunately, the waiter had returned and was, at that moment, placing a dish full of shrimp sauce on the table. When Alex banged on the table with her fist, the dish bounced into the air splattering sauce all over everywhere before it landed SPLAT! upside down on the table.

"ALEX!" Father and Mother exclaimed at the same time.

"Oops, sorry," Alex gasped. She wanted to hide under the table again or, better than that, run outside and never come back.

Father grabbed Alex by the arm as if guessing her wish to escape. As it turned out, the family had to move to a nearby table so that the waiter could clean the soiled tablecloth.

"Boy, Alex, they're really gonna hate you

around here," cackled Rudy, hardly able to control his giggles.

"Ahem," Father cleared his throat. "I guess it's too late to pretend you are not my daughter," he said to Alex.

"Dad!" Alex moaned. She hid her face in her hands.

The waiter returned with a second bowl of sauce. Alex did not look at him or at anyone else throughout the meal.

When it was time to go, Alex got up and followed her parents and Rudy out of the door. All at once, a sudden wave of arms and legs pressed in all around Alex. She felt an elbow jab her ribs. "What a slob!" someone hissed in her ear. And then they were gone.

Alex choked back tears as she watched the gang of girls skip merrily down the path. Of course, it had been Lisa and her friends.

A tap on her shoulder made Alex jump. She whirled around with her fists clenched, ready to fight it out with whoever stood there.

"Hey, take it easy," said Bryan Anderson.

"Oh, uh, sorry." Alex relaxed her fists.

"Aren't you getting tired of those dorky girls pushing you around?" asked Bryan.

"Sure," Alex replied, "but what can I do?"

"I've got an idea," Bryan told her. "Let's get Rudy and I'll explain it to both of you."

Bryan led Alex and Rudy to a spot farther down the shore, away from the swimming beach. Alex held her nose. The spot was covered with old, dead fish rotting in the sun.

"How do you think Lisa and Emily would like a few rotten fish heads in their beds tonight?" Bryan asked with a sly grin.

"Oh, no!" Alex laughed. "That would be too horrible. We couldn't do that, could we?" She chuckled at the thought.

"Why not?" Bryan shrugged his shoulders. "They have been really creepy to you, haven't they? Well, now's your chance to get them back. What do you say?"

Alex hesitated. "How would you get the fish heads into their beds without being seen?"

"Oh, that's simple," Bryan explained. "You sneak into the cottages when everyone else is down at the beach."

Alex wavered. She knew it wasn't the right thing to do, but those girls were such jerks. They deserved a few fish heads in their beds. And besides, it would be so funny!

"Okay, let's do it!" Alex decided.

"Oh, boy!" Rudy rubbed his hands together in excitement. Bryan ran to his cottage to get a few things that they would need. He returned with some newspaper and two large grocery sacks.

"What are you going to do?" Rudy asked him.

"I'm going to wrap the fish heads up in newspaper," Bryan answered. "That way they won't stink so much—in case somebody stops us along the way."

As Alex watched Bryan use a pocketknife to separate the heads from the bodies of the fish, she got the feeling that Bryan had done this sort of thing before.

After wrapping the heads in several layers of newspaper, Bryan put a bundle into each sack. Then he hid them in the bushes.

"Come on." He motioned for Alex and Rudy to follow him.

"What about the sacks?" Alex asked.

"We can't do it yet," Bryan replied. "It's too early. We need to wait until later this evening when everyone is at the beach. Then we'll sneak away when no one's looking."

Alex and Rudy hurried back to their cabin to change into their swimming suits. Bryan did the same. They met a few minutes later on the swimming beach.

"Just make it look like we are here to swim like everybody else," Bryan whispered.

73

They jumped into the water and paddled about. They made extra loud noises so that their parents would notice them in the water. Alex saw that the group of girls was watching her and this time she was glad. Let them watch her all they wanted. Tonight she would get her revenge!

Alex swam lazily about the swimming area. She dove off the dock with Rudy and Bryan and participated in a few air mattress races. She waved to her mother and father and to Barbara and Matt.

Finally, Bryan gave the signal. One by one, the three children sneaked off in different directions, being careful that no one saw them leave the swimming area together.

Alex's heart pounded with excitement. This was it! Lisa and Emily were really going to get it now!

CHAPTER 7

Fish Heads in Bed

"We better hurry," Bryan told Alex and Rudy as they made their way along the hilly path up to the cottages. "It's gonna get dark soon and people will be going back to their cottages."

"Right," Alex agreed. She hoped the sack full of fish heads that she was carrying would not tear and fall apart. It would be messy trying to scoop them off the path.

Soon, the children left the path and ducked behind some bushes at the side of a cottage.

"This is Emily's cottage," Bryan said in a low voice. "Go on," he told Alex. "Go put the fish heads in her bed."

"Me?" Alex cried in a panic. "But . . . but how do I do it?"

"Easy!" Bryan declared. "Just pull back the covers and let them fall into the bed. Try and get them pretty far down so Emily won't notice them until after she gets into bed. Then cover 'em back up."

Alex sniggered. How well she remembered Emily's cruel teasing when she had tried to water-ski this afternoon. Wouldn't the haughty look disappear from Emily's face when she crawled into bed with a bunch of smelly old fish heads?

"But how do I know which bedroom is Emily's?" Alex asked.

"Oh, you'll be able to tell," Bryan told Alex. "She's the only kid in the family."

"But what if someone sees me?" Alex hesitated once more. "I mean, what if I get caught?"

"Don't worry," Bryan assured her. "Rudy and I will keep watch."

Alex shrugged. She had run out of questions. She had better get the job done.

On tiptoe, Alex crossed the front porch of Emily's cottage. She cautiously pulled on the screen door. It opened easily.

"Hurry up!" Bryan hissed at her from behind the bushes.

Alex took a deep breath and stepped inside the cottage. She hurried through the rooms, looking for Emily's bedroom.

Now I know what a burglar feels like, she told herself. With every step, Alex felt more and more uneasy. *This is wrong,* she admitted to herself. *No matter how mean someone is to me, it's wrong to go sneaking through their cottage.*

She was just about to go back outside and tell Bryan and Rudy to forget the whole idea when she heard voices directly outside the cottage. Alex froze in fright. Those were not Bryan's and Rudy's voices. Those were girls' voices. It was Emily and Lisa!

The voices were on the front porch now and getting louder every second. Panicky, Alex looked around for a place to hide. Running into a bedroom, she dove inside a closet just as Emily and Lisa entered the cottage.

"Can I really wear your big hoop earrings?" Alex heard Lisa ask loudly.

"Oh, sure," answered Emily's voice. "They are in my room on the dresser."

Footsteps sounded louder and louder until the girls entered the same room as Alex. Squinting through a crack in the closet, Alex could see Lisa fiddling with pieces of jewelry that lay on top of a dresser. The dresser stood right beside the closet. Had the closet door been open, Alex could have reached out and touched Lisa.

"What do you think?" Emily's voice broke the silence. "Do you like my new T-shirt?"

Alex squinted through the crack with her other eye and saw Emily hold up a bright pink T-shirt for Lisa to admire.

"Ooooooh, that's cute," Lisa responded. "Are you going to wear it tonight?"

"Yes," Emily replied. She began to change her clothes.

Alex politely withdrew her gaze from the crack. She felt even more like a criminal. What would the girls do if they found her hiding in Emily's closet with a sack full of fish heads?

"Does it smell a little fishy in here?" Alex heard Lisa ask Emily.

"Maybe a little," came Emily's reply. "I'm sure my dad went fishing today. He probably left his smelly fishing junk inside."

"Peee-uuuu! Maybe he left the fish inside," Lisa responded. "Oh!" she suddenly cried. "One of the earrings rolled under the closet door!"

"Well, go get it!" Emily responded.

Upon hearing those words, Alex felt her heart pound loudly. She quickly looked around for a place to hide inside the closet.

"Get my earring," Emily repeated to Lisa.

Somehow, seconds before Lisa opened the closet door, Alex and the fish heads managed to disappear behind a half-blown air mattress that had been stuck in the corner of the closet. She tensed as Lisa's hand groped closer and closer to the air mattress.

"Got it!" Lisa suddenly shouted.

Alex gave a silent sigh of relief when Lisa left the closet, banging the door shut behind her. That had been a close call.

Alex wished the girls would hurry up and leave the cottage. She wanted to get out of the closet. It was horrible being stuck in there with the fish heads. Then Lisa said something that made Alex forget all about the smell.

"Wasn't it funny when Alex fell in the water today?" Lisa asked Emily.

"Oh yeah," Emily laughed. "That was so hilarious!"

The two girls laughed uproariously. Alex fumed to herself. It was all she could do to keep from bursting out of the closet and showing Emily and Lisa what she thought of their little joke. A couple of knocks on the head with a sack full of fish heads might teach them a thing or two!

"Come on, let's go," Lisa suddenly said.

"Okay," Emily replied. "You know, you are right—it does smell awfully fishy in here."

Alex waited until she heard the slam of the screen door before she lurched out of the closet. She was so angry. The fish smell was so bad. Sweat poured down her face. She felt sick.

Staggering over to Emily's bed, Alex threw back the covers. She pulled the bundle of newspaper out of the sack and unwrapped the

fishheads. Glazed eyeballs stared up at her.

Alex flung the heads off of the newspaper onto Emily's bed. She buried them nice and deep in the covers. There! Let Emily laugh at her! She wished she could be there to see Emily's face tonight.

Alex hurried from the room and out the door of the cottage. Outside, she scanned the area for Rudy and Bryan. They were nowhere to be seen.

"Some lookouts!" Alex grumbled. She turned to go down the path.

"Alex! Over here!" a voice hissed through the trees. It was Bryan. He beckoned Alex to come to his and Rudy's hiding place in the trees.

"Did you do it?" he asked Alex eagerly.

"Of course." Alex acted insulted that Bryan had even asked.

"We thought you got caught when those girls went inside the cottage," Rudy told her.

"I hid in Emily's closet," Alex explained. She told the boys all that had happened inside the cottage including the girls' mean comments about Alex waterskiing.

"Those jerks!" Bryan exclaimed. "They deserve to have something even worse than fish heads in their beds."

"Yeah," Rudy agreed. "They deserve to have a dead whale in their beds."

Alex and Bryan laughed.

"We couldn't fit a whale into one of these cottages," Alex told her brother.

The three children left the hiding place in the trees and made their way along the path to the Anderson cottage. Lisa's bed was the next target.

"Won't the fish smell bother you tonight?" Alex asked Bryan. "After all, you are in the same cottage as Lisa."

"Naw," Bryan answered. "I plan to sleep on the front porch, so I won't smell a thing."

When they reached the cottage, Alex looked sternly at Bryan and Rudy. "This time you better warn me if anybody comes," she said.

"Oh, yeah, sorry 'bout that," the boys replied sheepishly. "We'll keep better watch this time."

Alex hurried inside the Anderson cottage. Once again, she felt like a burglar. But for some reason, it was easier to commit the crime the second time around. *Brussels sprouts,* she thought to herself. What if she became a full-time burglar? *Yuck,* she thought as she caught a whiff of the fish heads. *No way!* Not if she had to carry these awful things around with her.

Alex had no trouble finding Lisa's bedroom and dumping the second package full of fish heads under the bedspread of her bed. The smell was almost unbearable by now, and, for a moment, Alex felt sorry for the other members of the Anderson family. What would Matt think if he knew Barbara's younger sister had filled his cottage with the stink of rotten fish?

Alex joined Bryan and Rudy outside. They all breathed a sigh of relief that the job was done. Grabbing hold of one another's hands, they skipped down the path to the beach. Running onto the swimming dock, the three children jumped and splashed into the water.

Lisa and Emily were talking and laughing in the center of the group of girls. Alex noticed that Emily had on her new pink T-shirt. She wondered if they were talking about her and her waterskiing attempt.

Well, Alex told herself, *Lisa and Emily won't be so happy when they crawl into bed tonight. They won't be happy at all.*

Alex giggled and plunged under the water. Hundreds of little bubbles rose to the surface as Alex laughed and laughed and laughed.

CHAPTER 8

A Secret Swim

Alex had just settled down in the double bed that she shared with Barbara when an ear-splitting scream shattered the stillness of the night. Alex and Barbara sat up and stared at one another. Then they hurried out to the front porch. The rest of the family joined them.

"What was that?" Mother asked worriedly.

"Sounded like it came from the Anderson cottage," said Father. "Look." He pointed in that direction. "All the lights are on and people are running around outside."

"Maybe we ought to go over there and see what's going on," Mother suggested.

Father agreed. "You children stay here," he told Alex, Rudy, and Barbara.

Alex and Rudy waited until their parents had gone several yards down the path and their sister had gone back inside the cottage. Then they collapsed in giggles, rolling around and around, holding their aching stomachs.

Before they had time to recover from the first scream, a second scream, this time from the direction of Emily's cottage, pierced the air. Alex and Rudy burst into new fits of laughter.

"Hey, you guys," a voice suddenly hissed from the porch steps.

"Who's there?" Alex gasped and peered down the steps.

"It's me, Bryan," said the voice.

"Oh," Alex sighed in relief. "Come on up."

"I can't stay long," Bryan said as he bounded up the steps to join Alex and Rudy on the porch. "I gotta get back before they miss me."

"Tell us what happened," Alex demanded. "Did Lisa like the fish heads?"

Bryan laughed. "It worked perfectly," he said. "She was incredibly grossed out."

"Good," Alex chuckled. "Does your cottage smell very bad?"

Bryan held his nose in reply. "Nobody can stand being inside the cottage. We are all going to have to sleep somewhere else tonight."

"Uh-oh," Alex sighed. "Are your parents very mad?"

Bryan shrugged. "They'll get over it." He stood up. "I gotta get going before they miss me."

After Bryan left, Alex said to Rudy, "Maybe we shouldn't have done it. What if both families have to move out of their cottages?"

"Yeah," answered Rudy. "We could be in big trouble."

"All right, Alex and Rudy," a voice suddenly cried behind them, "I heard the whole thing!"

Brother and sister whirled around. Alex gulped. Barbara stood in the doorway, the light from the cottage spilling around her and onto the porch.

"You heard the whole thing?" Alex repeated dumbly.

"Uh, what thing?" Rudy said brightly, trying to look innocent.

Barbara narrowed her eyes at him. "You

know what I'm talking about," she replied.

"Are you going to tell Mom and Dad?" Alex asked anxiously.

"That depends," her sister said. "First, tell me exactly what you did."

Alex and Rudy told Barbara about the fish heads and how Alex had put them in Lisa's and Emily's beds. By the time they had told the whole story, Barbara was laughing.

"But we didn't mean to make everybody have to leave the cottages for the night," Alex told her sister. "We didn't know the smell would be that bad."

"You didn't think rotten fish heads would smell that bad?" Barbara giggled. She wiped the laughter tears from her eyes. "I won't tell Mom and Dad what you have done," Barbara finally told Alex. "I'll leave it up to you to decide whether or not you should tell them."

She turned to go back inside. "Just do me a favor," she called over her shoulder. "Don't tell anybody until after the vacation. I'd just die if Matt found out that my little sister and brother were responsible for stinking up his cabin."

At that moment, the children heard voices on the path outside the cottage. A few moments later, Father and Mother appeared. With them were Mr. and Mrs. Anderson and Bryan! Alex stared at Rudy in alarm.

"Oh, hello," Mother said to the children. "We are having overnight guests."

"We are?" Alex and Rudy exclaimed together.

"Yes," replied Mother. "Can you believe that someone put some nasty-smelling fish heads in Lisa Anderson's bed? Who would do such a thing? Anyway, the Anderson cottage smells too bad for anyone to sleep there tonight, so Mr. and Mrs. Anderson are going to sleep on our sofa bed. Bryan said he'd like to sleep in your room tonight, Rudy."

"Hurrah!" Rudy cried.

Everyone followed Mother inside. Father helped Mr. Anderson set up the sofa bed, while Mother and Mrs. Anderson got Bryan settled in Rudy's bedroom.

Alex returned to the bedroom that she shared with Barbara and climbed in on her side of the big double bed. Long after Barbara had fallen asleep, Alex was still awake. She could not stop the disturbing thoughts that raced through her mind. What would her parents say if they knew that she had been the one to put the fish heads in Lisa's bed? What would Lisa and Emily say? What would the group of girls do to her if they found out?

For what seemed like hours, Alex tossed and turned. Finally, she crawled out of bed and went to stand in front of the bedroom window.

A nice breeze floated in through the window. From where she stood, Alex could see the lake shimmering in the moonlight. It looked so quiet and peaceful. If only she could walk by the lake awhile, it might help to calm her troubled mind.

Why not? she thought. *Why not take a little walk by the lake—just for a few minutes?*

Running her fingers along the bottom of the window, Alex found the hook that fastened the screen to the windowsill. Carefully, she pulled the hook out of the fastener. It made a slight noise. Alex listened to make sure the noise had not awakened Barbara.

Sure that her sister was sound asleep, Alex crawled up on the window ledge. She peered down at the ground below. It was too dark. She could not see a thing.

Holding her breath and silently counting, "One, two, three," Alex pushed herself off the ledge. She fought the urge to scream as she fell through black space. Then, OUCH! she hit bottom, right on top of a small but prickly bush.

Alex sat on the ground and rubbed her bruised body. She hoped no one had heard the rattling of the window screen or the crunch of the bush. After listening and hearing nothing from inside, Alex got up, brushed the dirt from her hands, and started down the path to the lake.

Upon reaching the beach area, Alex walked out on the long boardwalk that led to the diving dock. She lay down on her back at the end of the dock and stared at the stars.

There were so many stars! Alex gasped in wonder to think that God had made each and every one of them. And He had made a special place in the sky for each one of them, too. Why,

it seemed that He would have almost needed a map to make sure that He got the stars and the planets in the right places. She had not thought of it before, but making the heavens probably had been just as complicated as making the earth!

Suddenly, all thoughts of creation vanished. Alex heard a noise behind her. Spinning around, she spotted two figures creeping down the path to the beach. Lying flat against the dock, Alex held her breath. Who could they be?

The figures stopped at the edge of the water.

Alex could barely make out their outlines in the moonlight. They were not big enough to be grown-ups or teenagers. Could it be children her age?

Entering the water, the figures disappeared. Then all Alex could see were the dim outlines of two heads gliding across the water, coming closer and closer to the dock on which she was lying.

Finally, Alex heard one of the heads speak clearly, "Who could have put the fish heads in our beds, Lisa?"

"I don't know," the other head replied. "Maybe it was Alex."

Brussels sprouts! It was Lisa and Emily and they were now swimming right under the dock!

"Let's get up on the dock and dive in the water," Emily suggested.

Alex froze on the spot. If Lisa and Emily got up on the dock, she would be found out for sure.

Lisa seemed to be thinking it over. "No," she answered slowly. "Someone might hear the splash and catch us out here."

Alex breathed a quiet sigh of relief. She lay absolutely still. If she made even the tiniest of noises, the girls would know she was there.

For what seemed like hours, Alex listened to the splashes of the girls swimming below her. She cringed every time Emily tried to talk Lisa into climbing up on the diving dock. And she thanked God every time Lisa said "No" to Emily.

Just when Alex thought she could stand the secrecy no longer, a noise almost like a combined scream and a groan sounded below her.

"Lisa, what's the matter?" Emily's voice asked worriedly.

The groaning noise continued.

"Lisa! What's wrong?" This time Emily shouted.

Alex thought she heard Lisa mumble, "My leg . . . my leg . . ."

Then Emily screamed, "LISA! Stay above water! I can't hold you up!"

Alex hesitated. What should she do? Bubbly choking noises sounded below her. It sounded as if Lisa were drowning, and if someone didn't come to her rescue, Emily might drown with her!

"HELP! OH, SOMEBODY HELP ME!" came Emily's panic-stricken voice.

That was enough for Alex. Without waiting another second, she jumped into the water beside Emily.

Emily's eyes widened in surprise at Alex's sudden appearance at her side. But she did not bother to ask Alex where she had come from.

"Help me, Alex!" Emily pleaded. "Lisa is drowning!"

Alex quickly grabbed one of Lisa's arms to help keep her afloat. She remembered when she and Barbara had tried to hold Rudy up in the water. They had quickly lost their strength. She didn't think that she and Emily had any better chance of keeping Lisa above water.

"Lisa, you have to try and swim to shore," Alex shouted into the girl's ear.

"I can't," Lisa moaned and slipped under the water.

"LISA!" Emily screamed. With great effort, she and Alex raised the girl's head above water.

"What should we do?" Emily shouted to Alex.

"We need help," Alex cried. "HELP! HELP!" she began calling at the top of her voice.

"HELP! HELP!" Emily did the same.

All at once, a floodlight snapped on above them. It was wired to one of the posts on the dock. An emergency siren began screaming an alarm. Figures were running toward the beach from all directions.

"There's somebody out in the water!" someone shouted.

"Hurry up! We need to rescue them!" someone else cried.

"Alex! Is that you?" called Father, fear and panic in his voice.

Alex tried to answer but she did not have the strength to shout again. She had used all of her energy in trying to save Lisa.

"Oh, hurry up, Dad, please save me," Alex silently called to her father. Her legs and arms were so tired. She could not keep paddling much longer. Helplessly, Alex watched Lisa slip under water and, this time, Emily went with her. Alex struggled to keep herself afloat.

"Get Lisa and Emily," she gasped when her father reached her. There were men all about her now. She dimly recognized Mr. Anderson and Matt.

I wonder if anybody will be mad at us? was Alex's last thought before she collapsed in her father's arms.

CHAPTER 9

Rag Fight

A long dark tunnel lay before her. Someone at the other end of the tunnel was calling her name. "Alex, Alex!" She wanted to see who was calling her name, but she did not want to go through the tunnel. Bravely, she took a few steps into it. Immediately, the tunnel vanished and a bright light appeared.

Alex opened her eyes. She was lying on the beach. Her mother and father were bending over her. Their faces looked concerned.

"Alex," her mother said, smiling gently. Alex knew then that it had been her mother's voice that she had heard calling from the tunnel. "Oh, Alex," Mother cried as she lifted her daughter into a smothering hug. Father put his arms around both of them.

"Are Lisa and Emily all right?" Alex asked as soon as she was able.

"Yes, they are lying right next to you," answered her father.

Alex turned her head. Emily lay beside her and on the other side of Emily was Lisa. Their parents were also with them.

"Lisa has a terrible charley horse in her right leg," Mr. Anderson told them.

Alex knew what a charley horse was. It was a horrible cramp that a person got in the calf of his or her leg. It would usually happen when people over exercised. Alex sometimes got charley horses while playing sports.

"Is that why Lisa couldn't swim?" Alex asked.

"Yes," Mr. Anderson answered. "It's almost impossible to swim with a muscle cramp. That's why we only swim during the daytime when there are enough people around to help us if we get into trouble." Mr. Anderson looked sternly at his daughter.

"Yes, Dad," Lisa responded.

"You could have drowned out there tonight," Mrs. Anderson told her daughter.

"She would have drowned if it hadn't been for Alex," Emily declared suddenly.

Everyone stared at Emily and then at Alex.

"It's true, you know," Emily told Lisa. "I wouldn't have been able to keep you above water by myself."

Lisa gazed at Alex for a moment. "Thank you," she said softly.

"Oh, sure," Alex replied and shrugged as if saving someone's life was something she did every day.

"What I want to know," said Alex's father, "is why you girls were out here in the middle of the night?"

"Uh, Emily and I couldn't sleep," Lisa tried to explain. "It was too hot and stuffy in that little bedroom we are sharing."

"Yeah, we thought we could get cooled off in the lake," added Emily.

"It wouldn't have happened if we'd had our own bedrooms to sleep in," sniffed Lisa.

"Like we had before someone dumped fish heads all over our beds," grumbled Emily.

Alex squirmed uncomfortably. The excitement of tonight had almost made her forget about the fish heads. She wished now she had never pulled that prank.

"And why were you out here tonight, Alex?" Father asked with an odd little smile.

He knows! Alex gasped to herself. *He's smiling at me like he knows I put the fish heads in their beds!*

"Uh, I couldn't sleep either," Alex began. Staring into her father's eyes, she knew she had better confess what she had done. "I couldn't sleep because I was the one who put the fish heads in Lisa's and Emily's beds."

"You did?" Lisa exclaimed, jumping up angrily.

"What a rotten thing to do!" Emily shouted.

"Now hold on, girls," Mr. Anderson interrupted. "I would almost say that you deserved a few fish heads in your beds."

"Dad!" Lisa cried. "How could you say that?"

"Lisa," her father replied, "you and Emily and the whole group of girls have been terribly rude to Alex ever since she got here."

Lisa and Emily stared at Mr. Anderson with shocked faces. Alex quickly looked down at the ground. She was embarrassed.

"Don't think your actions have gone unnoticed," Mr. Anderson told his daughter. "It's hard to hide that kind of ugliness."

"I guess you're right, Dad," Lisa finally spoke. "We have been pretty creepy." She turned to Alex. "I'm sorry, Alex," she said.

"That's okay," replied Alex. "I'm sorry about the fish heads."

"Well," Emily said brightly, "you certainly made things exciting."

The grown-ups laughed.

Everyone soon returned to their cottages. Mr. and Mrs. Anderson walked ahead with Mother. Alex walked behind with her father. She had a few questions to ask him.

"Dad, did you really know that I put the fish heads in their beds?"

"I suspected so," Father answered. "You were the only person who had any reason to do it, Firecracker."

Alex took several more steps before asking, "Dad, how did you know that Lisa and Emily and I were in trouble tonight? Who woke you up?"

"Well, that was rather strange." Father rubbed his chin. "I woke up suddenly feeling that something was wrong, but I didn't know what it was. Then, I heard you and Emily call for help. I woke up George Anderson on my way out. He turned on the lights and the siren."

Alex thought for a moment. "Do you think God woke you up because I was in danger?"

"Yes, I think that is exactly what happened," Father decided. "For what other reason would I wake up just in time to save you?"

"Brussels sprouts," Alex breathed. "The Lord sure has rescued me a lot of times this vacation."

"Yes," Father agreed, "He led me right to you when you and Rudy were lost, and He helped me pull you out of the water when you were water-skiing."

"And then He woke you up in time to rescue me tonight," Alex added. "Do you think the

Lord will ever get tired of having to rescue me?" she asked anxiously.

"No, Firecracker," Father replied. "The Lord never gets tired of taking care of His children."

"But how about you, Dad?" Alex persisted. "Will you ever get tired of rescuing me?"

Father laughed his big, booming laugh. "No, Firecracker, I will not get tired of rescuing you either. Now, let's go back to bed!"

The next morning, Rudy and Bryan confessed their parts in the fish heads crime. A little before noon, Alex, Rudy, and Bryan marched down the path behind Father and Mr. Anderson. They were on their way to the Anderson cottage. They carried with them a mop, several rags, soap, and two scrub buckets.

When they got there, Lisa and Emily were sitting on the front porch, waiting for them.

"Why do we have to help clean the cottage?" Lisa complained.

"Yeah," Emily grumbled, "we didn't put the fish heads inside."

"This whole thing wouldn't have happened if you girls had been nice to Alex," Mr. Anderson replied sternly. He led the way into the cottage. They all followed after him.

Alex sniffed the air of the cottage. It didn't smell too bad in the front part of the cottage. But in walking to the back of the cottage, and especially in Lisa's bedroom, it smelled awfully fishy.

"You need to wash the walls and the floor in Lisa's room," Mr. Anderson told the girls. "Two of you can do the walls and one of you can mop the floor. That should take care of the fish odor.''

Father and Mr. Anderson showed the girls how to fill the buckets with the right amount of soap and water. Then they took Rudy and Bryan with them to clean Emily's cottage.

"I'm not going to clean anything,'' Emily declared after the men had gone.

"Oh, yes, you are,'' Lisa told her friend. "My dad is not going to let us out of here until the fish smell is gone and the only way to do that is to clean my bedroom!''

Lisa dragged Emily into her bedroom. Alex followed. She was uneasy. Even though Lisa and Emily had been friendly last night, she wasn't sure that they would be so today, especially now that they knew she was responsible for the fish heads.

At first, the girls did not talk much to one another. They were too busy cleaning the room. Lisa and Emily washed the walls. Alex scrubbed the floor.

Having watched her mother scrub the kitchen floor many times in the past, Alex thought she knew how to use a mop. However, before long, water was standing all over the floor.

"Hey!" cried Emily to Alex. "Don't you know you are supposed to wring the water out of the mop as you go along?"

"Oh, yeah," Alex said, grinning. "I knew I was forgetting something."

"Just for that, you get a soapy rag in the face!" Emily cried. She threw her wet rag at Alex, catching her squarely on the chin.

"Yuck!" Alex hollered and flung the rag back at Emily. She hit her in the stomach, causing a big wet blotch to appear on Emily's T-shirt.

"Now you're really gonna get it!" Emily laughed. She dunked her rag in the bucket to get it nice and wet. But before she could throw it at Alex, Lisa hurled her rag at Emily, making another wet blotch on the back of Emily's shirt.

"Ahhhhhh!" Emily cried and threw the rag back at Lisa. All thoughts of cleaning disappeared as the girls battled each other with wet rags. Somehow, in the middle of things, Alex's scrub bucket was knocked over and the water spilled. A small river ran through Lisa's bedroom. In a matter of minutes, the room had turned into a disaster.

The girls finally collapsed in giggles. They were, by now, as wet as the floor.

"Well, that was a great way to clean a room!" Emily gasped.

"Yeah," Alex agreed. "Let's go clean another one!"

The girls laughed.

"You know, Alex," said Lisa, "you are a fun person to be with."

"Yeah, Alex," Emily nodded, looking down at her wet clothes. "You sure throw a mean rag!"

Emily picked up a rag and tossed it at Alex. Alex threw it back at Emily, and with that, the rag fight began all over again.

CHAPTER 10

Beach Party

It was the last day of vacation at Crawdad Cove and everyone was getting ready for the beach party that evening. Alex, Rudy, and Barbara were watching the men set up tables on the swimming beach for the picnic. Alex laughed as she watched her father. He looked so funny in his long, multicolored shorts and bright red shirt. A round sailor's cap perched on his head.

Suddenly, Alex caught sight of the park ranger who had been with Father the night that she and Rudy had been lost. He was walking along the beach and with him was the wolf-dog!

Alex ran to the beach. Rudy and Barbara followed. The park ranger smiled when he saw them.

"Where did you find him?" Alex asked the ranger. She knelt down beside the big animal and put her arms around his neck.

"He was right at the same place where we found you and your brother," the ranger told Alex. "I went back there the next day. He seemed to want to come with me."

"Are you going to keep him?" Alex asked.

"I think I will," answered the ranger. He reached down and scratched the wolf-dog's ears.

Alex and Rudy said good-bye to the wolf-dog and watched as it and the ranger moved on down the beach. Alex was glad that the animal now had a good home.

"I can't believe the week is almost gone and that we go home tomorrow," Barbara said with a sudden sigh. "It seems like we just got here. Don't you agree?"

"Yes and no," Alex replied slowly. "Some parts of the week seemed to last a long, long time. When Rudy and I were lost, it felt like we were lost forever. But the last three days have just zoomed by."

Alex smiled to herself. She had been doing fun things with Lisa and Emily the last three days. Who would have thought that a friendship could be started by a few fish heads and a rag fight? But ever since the day the three girls had flung wet, soapy rags at each other, Lisa, Emily, and Alex had become good friends. They had gone waterskiing several times, and Alex was getting better each time. She could even jump over the waves at the back of the boat.

But, although she and Lisa and Emily were friends, the other girls in the group did not show any desire to become friends with Alex. Indeed, they were even more unfriendly than before. And to make matters worse, the group of girls would have nothing to do with Lisa and Emily now that they were friends with Alex.

One day, Alex told Lisa and Emily her father's story of the orchard and how one section of peach trees ate God's food, but the other section ate bad food. She told them how the peach trees that ate God's food grew big, juicy peaches, but the trees that ate the bad food only grew pits.

When Alex had finished, Lisa had exclaimed, "You know, that's right! I used to think that the most important thing on earth was to be popular—you know, hang around with the popular kids, wear the same kind of clothes, and listen to the same kind of music. But now I know that other things are a lot more important—like being kind to other people. And you know what? I feel better! I feel a lot better about myself because I know I'm doing the right thing."

"Right," said Alex. "You're producing good fruit."

"You're not hanging around the pits anymore," Emily had added. And they had all laughed.

Alex was remembering that conversation as she stared at the swimming dock. There they were—the whole group of girls—lined up along the swimming dock. Each of them had on a short knit skirt and top, matching socks, and white tennis shoes.

I wonder if they have to ask each other how to think? Alex asked herself.

Her thoughts, however, were suddenly interrupted when someone shouted over the loud-speaker, "SURF'S UP!"

"HURRAH!" all the children cried. They ran down to the water's edge to a big pile of surfboards. Picking up boards, the children carried them into the water and got ready to race each other. They were going to see who would be the fastest to paddle a surfboard around a buoy set several yards out in the water.

Alex grabbed a blue board and ran to the water. She lay flat on the board on her stomach and waited for the race to begin. She looked around. Rudy and Bryan were next to her with their boards, and on the other side were Lisa and Emily.

"On your mark, get set, BANG!" The starting gun went off and so did the children.

Alex paddled furiously with her hands and kicked hard with her feet. She pulled ahead of most of the children but could not pass Bryan. Then, over her left shoulder, Alex caught a glimpse of Lisa, rapidly catching up with them.

Alex and Bryan made the turn around the buoy together and might have sped safely off

toward the finish line, except that Lisa rammed her surfboard into the tail end of Bryan's, causing him to flip over into Alex. Alex rolled off her board into the water. Other children and other boards crashed into Bryan, Alex, and Lisa until they had what looked like a snarled traffic jam in the water.

No one cared. Everyone laughed. Alex, Bryan, and Lisa got the booby prize for causing such a mess. They laughed until they cried when they saw what it was—a green plastic fish head with a hook in its mouth.

"Here, Alex," Lisa giggled, handing Alex the fish head. "You should keep this always—in memory of Crawdad Cove!"

"Thanks," Alex replied. "I think I will."

The next event was sand volleyball and then there was a tug of war. Alex and Mr. Anderson were on the opposite team from Father and Rudy. Father got pulled into the lake and his team lost. Alex laughed.

Looking over at the swimming dock, Alex noticed that the group of girls were still there. They stood on the dock in their matched outfits.

"Aren't those girls going to do anything at the beach party?" Alex asked Lisa and Emily.

"No," Lisa replied. "They will just stand there the whole time and look bored."

"Really?" Alex asked. "Why?"

"They think they're cool," Emily said.

"Well, if that's being cool, you can forget it," answered Alex. "I'd rather have fun."

"Me, too," Lisa agreed. "Come on, they're having a watermelon seed spitting contest!" She pointed at a crowd of people on the other side of the swimming dock.

"Now, Alex, what you do," Lisa began to explain when they reached the seed-spitting event, "is to grab a chunk of watermelon and start spitting the seeds as far as you can across that line over there. The person who spits a seed the farthest wins."

"On your mark, get set, go!"

Alex grabbed a big piece of watermelon and began chewing. She was just about to spit her first seed when a chorus of shrill screams cut through the air.

Everyone stopped what they were doing and looked in the direction of the swimming dock. The girls who had been standing on the dock no longer looked bored. In fact, they looked frightened out of their wits. Some of them were jumping up and down on the dock, but most of them were plunging into the water, short skirts, matching socks, and all. They screamed at the top of their lungs.

"What's going on?" Alex wondered.

"Beats me," Emily shrugged.

"Let's go find out," Lisa suggested.

The three girls ran to the dock and moved to

the spot where the other girls had stood only moments before.

"Don't go any closer," one of the girls warned them. "There's a snake up there!"

"A snake?" Lisa frowned. "Where?"

"I see it," Emily pointed. "Over there."

Alex looked. She crept cautiously forward and looked again. What she saw made her smile.

"Better not go any closer," the girl warned again.

"Oh, don't worry," Alex told the girl. "I know how to handle snakes like these."

"Alex!" Lisa cried. "Watch out! You could get bitten!"

"No problem," Alex assured her. And then, to everyone's dismay, she reached down, grabbed the snake by the throat, and held it up for them to see.

"Is it dead?" Emily asked as the snake made no movement.

"Well, in a way I guess it's dead," Alex chuckled. "It never was alive. It's my brother's rubber snake."

Emily and Lisa burst out laughing.

"It's a rubber snake!" they called with glee to the girls in the water. The girls, of course, did not share Emily and Lisa's laughter. They struggled from the water with embarrassed faces and very wet clothes.

Alex, Emily, and Lisa sat on the dock and laughed until their stomachs hurt.

"Well, so much for worldly popularity," chuckled Alex.

"It sure can be the pits," laughed Lisa.

"Peach pits, that is," added Emily. And they laughed and laughed.

Amen.

SHOELACES AND BRUSSELS SPROUTS

One little lie, but BIG trouble!

When Alex lies to her mom about losing her shoelaces, it doesn't seem like a big deal. But how do you replace special baseball laces when you don't have any money and you're not allowed to go to the store alone? A big softball game is coming up, and Alex knows the coach won't let her pitch in shoes without laces—or in cowboy boots!

Every kid gets into the predicaments that Alex does—ones that start out small and mushroom. Readers will learn from Alex's mistakes and understand that they have the same sources of help that she turns to: A God who loves them and wants to help them, and parents who understand.

Other books in the Alex Series . . .

2 *French Fry Forgiveness*—Sometimes making friends is harder than making enemies.

3 *Hot Chocolate Friendship*—Is winning first place as important to Alex as being a friend?

4 *Peanut Butter and Jelly Secrets*—Obeying her parents (even in little things) beats the awful results of disobeying.

Available at your local Christian bookstore.

David C. Cook Publishing Co.
850 N. Grove Ave.
Elgin, IL 60120

FRENCH FRY FORGIVENESS

Two Alexandrias!

Alex (short for Alexandria) expects to make new friends when she joins the swim team—but she doesn't count on meeting *another* Alexandria! How can she make friends with Alexandria, who pushes her into the pool for no reason?

Alex knows she should forgive Alexandria, but that seems impossible! Is there *anything* Alex can do to win Alexandria's friendship?

Every kid gets into the predicaments that Alex does—ones that start out small and mushroom. Readers will learn from Alex's mistakes and understand that they have the same sources of help that she turns to: A God who loves them and wants to help them, and parents who understand.

Other books in the Alex Series . . .

1 *Shoelaces and Brussels Sprouts*—It's always better to tell the truth, as Alex learns the hard way.

3 *Hot Chocolate Friendship*—Is winning first place as important to Alex as being a friend?

4 *Peanut Butter and Jelly Secrets*—Obeying her parents (even in little things) beats the awful results of disobeying.

NANCY LEVENE, who shares Alex's love of softball, lives with her husband and daughter in Kansas.

HOT CHOCOLATE
FRIENDSHIP

The worst possible partner!

That's who Alex gets for the biggest project of the school year. She won't have a chance at first place if she has to work with Eric Linden. He's the slowest kid in third grade.

Alex can't understand why he has to be her partner. Is she supposed to share God's love with Eric? Could that be more important than winning first place?

Every kid gets into the predicaments that Alex does—ones that start out small and mushroom. Readers will learn from Alex's mistakes and understand that they have the same sources of help that she turns to: A God who loves them and wants to help them, and parents who understand.

Other books in the Alex Series . . .

1 *Shoelaces and Brussels Sprouts*—It's always better to tell the truth, as Alex learns the hard way.
2 *French Fry Forgiveness*—Sometimes making friends is harder than making enemies.
4 *Peanut Butter and Jelly Secrets*—Obeying her parents (even in little things) beats the awful results of disobeying.

NANCY LEVENE, who shares Alex's love of softball, lives with her husband and daughter in Kansas.

PEANUT BUTTER AND JELLY SECRETS

Where did her money go?

Alex's mom *trusted* her with her school lunch money—and now it's gone! How will she ever get through the week without Mom *or* her teacher finding out? And what will she do when her class goes to lunch for the next five days?

Every kid gets into the predicaments that Alex does—ones that start out small and mushroom. Readers will learn from Alex's mistakes and understand that they have the same sources of help that she turns to: A God who loves them and wants to help them, and parents who understand.

Other books in the Alex Series . . .

1 *Shoelaces and Brussels Sprouts*—It's always better to tell the truth, as Alex learns the hard way.

2 *French Fry Forgiveness*—Sometimes making friends is harder than making enemies.

3 *Hot Chocolate Friendship*—Is winning first place as important to Alex as being a friend?

NANCY LEVENE, who shares Alex's love of softball, lives with her husband and daughter in Kansas.

CHERRY COLA CHAMPIONS

It's soccer season!

Alex can't imagine anyone not loving soccer until Lorraine joins her team. Lorraine can't run or kick. And no one wants to play with her.

How does that make Lorraine feel? Alex wonders. . . . But watch out when Alex decides to teach Lorraine soccer! Then maybe the kids will like Lorraine better. How can she lose with Alex as her coach?

Every kid gets into the predicaments that Alex does—ones that start out small and mushroom. Readers will learn from Alex's mistakes and understand that they have the same sources of help that she turns to: A God who loves them and parents who understand.

More books in the Alex series . . .

Mint Cookie Miracles (About Prayer)
Cherry Cola Champions
  (About Compassion)
The Salty Scarecrow Solution
  (About Unselfishness)
Peach Pit Popularity (About Friendship)

NANCY LEVENE, who shares Alex's love of softball, lives in Kansas.

Available at your local Christian bookstore.

THE KIDS FROM APPLE STREET CHURCH

How did it happen?

Every day brings new excitement in the lives of Mary Jo, Danny, and the other kids from Apple Street Church. Whether it's finding a stolen doll in a coat sleeve, chasing important papers all over the school yard, meeting a famous astronaut, or discovering the real truth about a mysteriously broken leg, the kids write it all in their personal notebooks to God.

Usually diaries are private. But this is your chance to look over the shoulders of The Kids from Apple Street Church as they tell God about their secret thoughts, their problems, and their fun times. It's just like praying, except they are writing to God instead of talking to Him.

Don't miss any of the adventures of The Kids from Apple Street Church!

1. Mary Jo Bennett
2. Danny Petrowski
3. Julie Chang
4. Pug McConnell
5. Becky Garcia
6. Curtis Anderson

Available at your local Christian bookstore.

David C. Cook Publishing Co.
850 N. Grove Ave.
Elgin, IL 60120

Are you looking for fun ways to bring the Bible to life in the lives of your children?

Chariot Family Publishing has hundreds of books, toys, games, and videos that help teach your children the Bible and apply it to their everyday lives.

Look for these educational, inspirational, and fun products at your local Christian bookstore.